THE RUSSIAN FAIRY BOOK

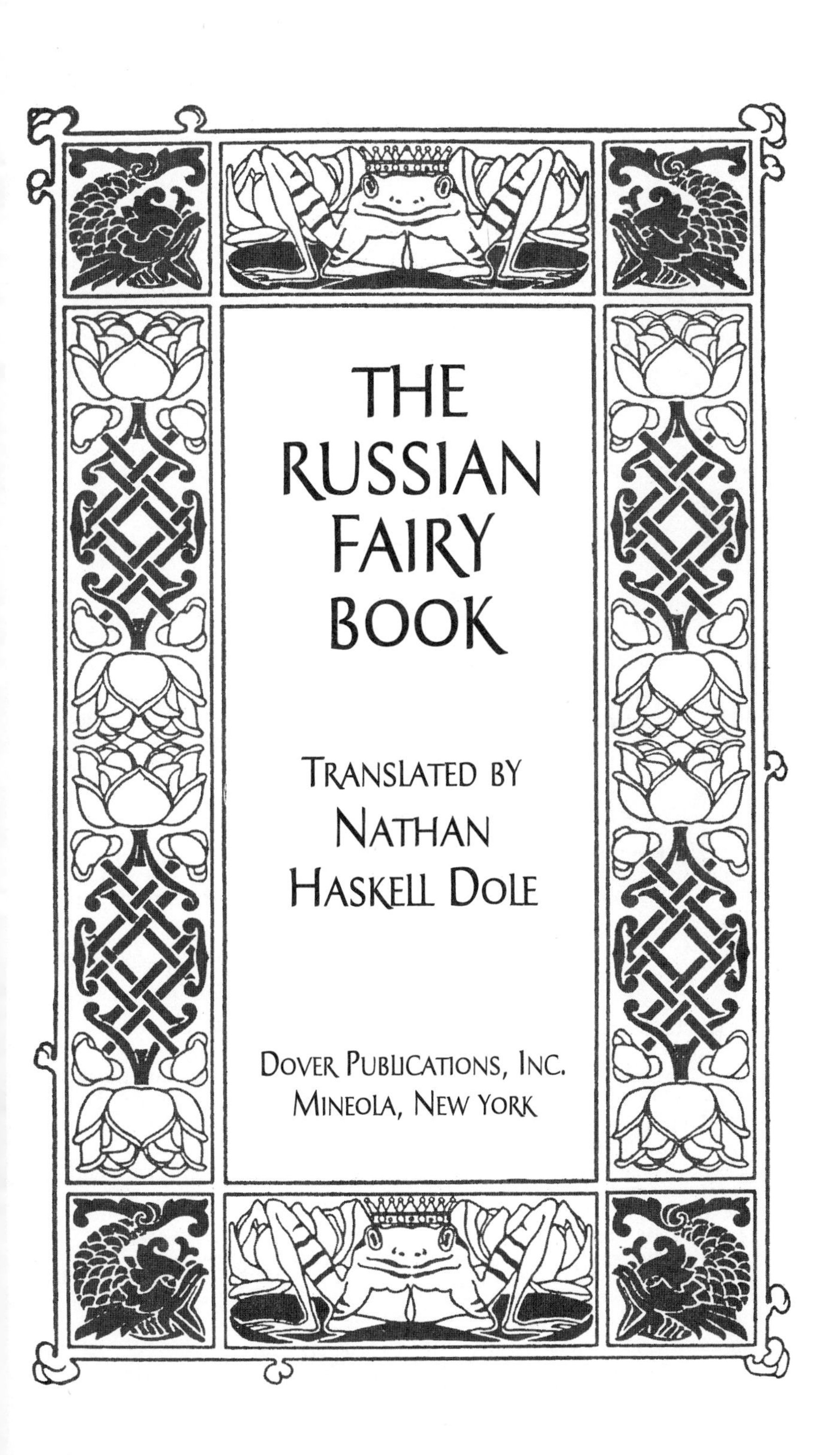

THE RUSSIAN FAIRY BOOK

TRANSLATED BY
NATHAN HASKELL DOLE

DOVER PUBLICATIONS, INC.
MINEOLA, NEW YORK

Published in Canada by General Publishing Company, Ltd., 30 Lesmill Road, Don Mills, Toronto, Ontario.

Bibliographical Note

This Dover edition, first published in 2000, is an unabridged republication of the work published by Thomas Y. Crowell & Co., Cambridge, Mass. in 1907. The illustrations from that work have been omitted and two minor typographical errors have been corrected for this edition.

Library of Congress Cataloging-in-Publication Data

The Russian fairy book / translated by Nathan Haskell Dole.
p. cm.
Contents: Vasilisa the beauty—The bright-hawk's feather—Ivan and the gray wolf—The little sister and little brother—The white duckling—Marya Morevna—The frog-queen.
ISBN 0-486-41019-6
1. Fairy tales—Russia. 2. Tales—Russia. [1. Fairy tales. 2. Folklore—Russia.] I. Dole, Nathan Haskell, 1852–1935.

PZ8 .R8974 2000
398.2'0947—dc21

99-088108

Manufactured in the United States of America
Dover Publications, Inc., 31 East 2nd Street, Mineola, N.Y. 11501

CONTENTS

THE RUSSIAN FAIRY BOOK

VASILISA THE BEAUTY

NCE in a certain country lived a merchant. He had been married twelve years and had only one child, a daughter Vasilisa, whom everyone called Vasilisa the Beauty. When her mother died the little girl was eight years old. On her deathbed she called her young daughter to her, took out from under the bedclothes a Doll, gave it to her, and said:

"Listen, dear little Vasilisa! Remember and fulfil my last words. I am dying and I leave you, with a mother's blessing, this Doll. Keep it always with you and show it to no one, and whenever any misfortune happens to you give it something to eat and ask its advice." Thereupon the mother kissed her little daughter and died.

The merchant, after his wife's death, mourned as long as was reasonable, and then began to think about getting married again. He was a good, sensible man and did not concern himself with the maidens, but best of all he liked a certain young widow. She knew about children, had two daughters of her own about the same age as Vasilisa, and, of course, could keep house and do all that a mother should do.

The merchant married the widow, but he made a mistake: he did not find in her a good mother for his child. Vasilisa was the prettiest girl in the whole village, and the stepmother and the stepsisters were envious of her beauty. They treated her cruelly and made her do impossible tasks, so that she might grow thin under the burden and her complexion might turn dark under the wind and sun. Indeed, it was no life at all for her!

But Vasilisa bore it uncomplainingly, and every day she grew more beautiful and plump than ever, while her stepmother and stepsisters grew uglier and thinner from ill-temper, in spite of the fact that they never did anything but sit round with folded hands like fine ladies. How did this happen?

Vasilisa's Doll helped her. Had it not been for that the poor girl could not have stood so much work.

Vasilisa did not eat the daintiest morsels of her scanty fare, but she used to put them aside for her little Doll, and in the evening when the rest had gone to bed she would shut herself into her little room and give it the good things, saying:

"Here, little Doll, eat something and listen to my tale of woe! Here I live in my papa's house, but I do not get any pleasure out of it. My wicked stepmother is trying to drive me out of the bright world. Teach me! How must I behave and what must I do?"

The Doll would eat a little and then give her good advice and console her for her sorrow, and before morning came it would finish every one of Vasilisa's tasks. While she was resting in the cool air or gathering flowers, the beds were weeded for her, the cabbages watered, the pails filled, and the fire made. The Doll also taught her how to avoid sunburn. It was fine to live with the Doll!

Several years passed. Vasilisa had grown up into a beautiful maiden. All the young men in town sought her, though not one of them would so much as look at her stepsisters. The stepmother was crosser than ever and replied to all the suitors: "We will not give the youngest one before the older ones."

And as soon as she had sent the suitors away she would vent her spite on Vasilisa with blows.

Now it happened that the merchant was obliged

to go away from home for a long time on important business. The stepmother went to live in another house which stood near a dense forest, and in this was a hut where Baba Yaga the Witch dwelt. She was a wicked hag who never permitted any person to approach her, and she ate men like chickens.

Having settled in her new home, the merchant's wife kept inventing pretexts to send the detested Vasilisa into the forest, but the girl always came back without accident. The Doll showed her the way and did not let her go near the Baba Yaga's hut.

Autumn came. The stepmother one time gave the three girls their evening's work to do: she bade one to make woven lace, and the second to knit stockings, but she set Vasilisa to spinning. She put out the lights throughout the house and left only one little candle where the girls were working, and she herself went to bed. While the girls were working the candle began to gutter. One of the girls took the snuffers to trim the wick, but instead of doing so she followed her mother's directions and, as if accidentally, put out the candle.

"Now what are we going to do?" asked the girls. "There is not a light in the whole house and our stints are not finished! We must go to the Baba Yaga after a light."

"I have all the light I want from my bosom-pin," said the one who was working on the lace; "I won't go."

"And I won't go," said the one who was knitting stockings; "I have enough light from my knitting needles."

"Vasilisa must go after the light," cried both of them. "Hurry to Baba Yaga the Witch and get it!" And they drove her out of the room.

Vasilisa went into her little room, set before her Doll the supper that she had saved for her, and said:

"Now, Dollie, take your supper and listen to my tale of woe. They are sending me to the Baba Yaga after fire, and the Baba Yaga will eat me!"

The Doll ate the food and her eyes gleamed like two candles. "Do not be afraid, little Vasilisa," she said. "Go whither they send you; only keep me always with you. When you have me you have nothing to fear at the Witch's hut."

So Vasilisa made haste, hid the Doll in her pocket, and having crossed herself went into the dense forest. As she went along tremblingly a horseman suddenly galloped past her. He was white, his dress was white, the horse he rode was white, and the horse's trappings were white. Outdoors it began to grow light.

She walked farther, and another horseman galloped past. He was red, his clothing was red, and he rode a red horse. The sun began to rise.

Vasilisa walked all night and all day, and only toward the next evening did she reach the clearing where stood the Baba Yaga's hut. The fence around the hut was of men's bones, and the posts were decorated with human skulls. Instead of door-posts were men's leg-bones; instead of shutters were arms; instead of a lock was a mouth with sharp teeth.

Vasilisa was benumbed with terror and stood as if rooted to the spot. Suddenly another horseman came riding along. He was black, his clothing was black, and he rode a black horse. He galloped up to the Baba Yaga's gates and disappeared as if he had sunk through the earth. Night had come. But the darkness did not last long. In the skulls on the fence the eyes gleamed, and it was as light as noon all over the clearing. Vasilisa shook with terror, but not knowing where to run she remained where she was.

Soon a terrible noise was heard in the forest. The trees trembled and the dry leaves rustled. It was the Baba Yaga coming. She stormed along in a mortar, she whipped it up with her pestle, she swept away the tracks with her besom. She came up to the gates, paused, and sniffing all around cried out: "Fu! fu! fu! I smell Russian breath! Who is here?"

Vasilisa approached the old dame with fear and trembling, and bowing low said: "It is I, grannie. My stepmother's daughters sent me to you to get some fire."

"Good!" exclaimed the Baba Yaga. "I know them. Live on, and do some work for me and then I will give you some fire; but if you do not do it, then I will eat you up."

She turned to the gates and cried: "Hey! my strong fence give way! Oh my high gates open!"

The gates opened and the Baba Yaga went in, and Vasilisa followed her, and then all was closed tight again. As soon as she entered the room the Baba Yaga stretched herself out and said to Vasilisa: "Bring me here what is on the stove; I want to eat."

Vasilisa lighted a splinter at the skulls' eyes on the fence and began to take down the food from the stove and give it to the Baba Yaga. There was enough for ten men. From the cellar she brought bread and meat, beer and wine. The old dame ate and drank, leaving for Vasilisa only a bit of soup, a crust of bread, and a morsel of roast pig.

Then the Baba Yaga lay down to sleep, saying: "When morning comes I am going out. Keep your eyes open, clean the court, sweep the hut, get the dinner, prepare the bedclothes; then go into the cornbin, take forty bushels of wheat and clean it of fennel. Have all this completely done, or I will eat you up."

After giving this command the Baba Yaga began to snore. Vasilisa put the old dame's leavings before the Doll, burst into tears, and said:

"Now eat, little Doll, and listen to my tale of woe! The Baba Yaga has given me such a heavy task to perform, and she threatens to eat me up if it is not all accomplished. Help me!"

The Doll replied: "Fear not, Vasilisa. Eat your supper, say your prayers, and go to sleep. Morning is wiser than Evening."

Vasilisa did so. She awoke rather early, but the Baba Yaga was up before her and was looking out of the window; the eyes in the skulls were growing dim, and now the white horseman galloped by and it became quite bright. The Baba Yaga went outdoors, whistled, and before her appeared her mortar and pestle and besom. The red horseman flashed by and the sun came up.

The Baba Yaga got into her mortar and started off. She spurred it on with the pestle and swept away the traces with her besom.

Vasilisa was left alone and she began to investigate the Baba Yaga's house. She was amazed at the abundance of everything, and she could not make up her mind which task she would take hold of first. But she soon discovered that her work was done for her already. The Doll was just separating out from the wheat the last grains of the fennel.

"Oh, you are my dear deliverer!" exclaimed Vasilisa. "You have saved me from misfortune!"

"All that is left for you to do is to get dinner," replied the Doll, climbing into Vasilisa's pocket. "Get it, and God be with you; but now take a good rest for your health."

Toward evening Vasilisa laid the table and waited for the Baba Yaga. It began to grow dark. The black horseman galloped by the gates. Then the eyes in the skulls began to gleam. The trees trembled, the leaves rustled — up came the Baba Yaga. Vasilisa met her. "Is your work all done?" asked the hag.

"You can see for yourself, grannie," replied Vasilisa.

The Baba Yaga looked all around, and became very angry because there was nothing to be angry about. "Very good!" she said sullenly; then she cried: "My faithful servants, my bosom friends, grind my wheat for me!" Instantly appeared three pairs of hands, seized the wheat, and carried it out of sight.

The Witch ate her supper, lay down to sleep, and again gave Vasilisa her orders.

"To-morrow do the same as you did to-day; but above all, take from the corncrib the poppy, and clean it of all dirt to the last seed. You'll cause trouble for someone if the least bit of earth is mixed with the poppy."

Then she turned her face to the wall and began to snore as before.

Vasilisa gave her Doll something to eat. The Doll ate and told her what she had told her the evening before:

"Pray to God and go to sleep; Morning is wiser than Evening; all shall be done, dear little Vasilisa!"

In the morning the Baba Yaga again flew away in her mortar, and Vasilisa and the Doll quickly accomplished the work that was to be done. In the evening the old hag came home, inspected everything, and cried out: "My faithful servants, my bosom friends, make some oil out of the poppy." Three pairs of hands appeared, seized the poppy, and carried it out of sight. The Baba Yaga sat down to supper, and while she ate, Vasilisa stood by in silence.

"Why don't you have something to say to me?" asked the Witch; "you stand there like one tongue-tied."

"I did not dare to," said Vasilisa; "but if you will allow me, I should like to ask you something."

"Ask away! Only remember — not every question leads to good! If you come to know too much you will quickly grow old."

"I only wanted to ask you about what I saw, grannie. As I was coming to you I was overtaken by a white horseman on a white horse in white clothes. Who is he?"

"That is my bright Day," said the Baba Yaga.

"Then I was overtaken by another horseman on a red horse. He was red and in red clothes. Who is he?"

"That is my red Sun," replied the Baba Yaga.

"And what was the meaning of the black horseman who overtook me just at your gates, grannie?"

"That was my black Night. All are my faithful servants."

Vasilisa remembered the three pairs of hands, but said nothing more.

"Why don't you ask something more?" demanded the Baba Yaga.

"I am afraid of what you said might happen to me: if one comes to know too much one grows old."

"It is good," said the Baba Yaga, "that you should ask only about what you have seen out of doors and not what you have seen in the house. I do not like people to tell tales about me out of school, and I eat up those who are too inquisitive! And now I am going to put a question to you. How did you succeed in doing the work which I gave you to do?"

"My mother's blessing helped me," replied Vasilisa.

"What is that? Begone from me, you daughter-with-the-blessing! I don't want people who have been blessed!"

And she dragged Vasilisa from the room and

pushed her out of the gates. Then she took down from the fence one of the skulls with the lighted eyes, put it on a stick, and gave it to her, saying: "Here is the light for your stepsisters. Take it! That is what they sent you here for."

Vasilisa hastened home on the run, by the light of the skull, and it did not go out till the next morning. At last toward the evening of the second day she reached her home. As she went through the gates she was going to throw the skull away.

"Why, of course," she said to herself, "they won't need the light now." But suddenly she heard a quiet voice from the skull saying: "Don't throw me away! Take me to your stepmother."

She looked up at her stepmother's house, and not seeing a light in any window, she resolved to go in with the skull. The first persons she met spoke kindly to her, and told her that since she had been away they had had no light in the house. They could n't make anything burn, and the fire which they tried to bring from the neighbours went out the moment it was brought into the house.

"Perhaps your light will keep!" said the stepmother. They carried the skull into the house, when the eyes gazed so steadily at the stepmother and her daughters that it burnt them. They tried to hide, but wherever they went the eyes always followed them. In the morning they were burnt to ashes, but it did not touch Vasilisa.

Then Vasilisa buried the skull in the ground, locked the house up, went into the city, and asked for shelter with an old woman who had no relations. She said to the old woman: "It is tiresome for me to have nothing to do, grannie. Come buy me the very best flax and I will spin for you."

The woman bought some of the very best flax and Vasilisa sat down to her task. The work fairly glowed under her hands and the thread that she made came out as smooth and even as hair. She made a lot of thread the finest that ever was seen. No one could equal it. Vasilisa had gone to ask her Doll's advice, and the Doll had said: "Bring me an old comb and an old shuttle, even a curry-comb: I will do it for you."

So Vasilisa got her all that she asked for, and went to bed; and the Doll during the night made a splendid loom.

Toward the end of the winter the linen was all spun, and it was so fine that one could pass it through the eye of a needle like a thread. In the spring they bleached the linen, and Vasilisa said to the old woman: "Grannie, take this linen and get some money for it!"

The old dame looked at the stuff and exclaimed: "No, my dear child, no one except the Tsar should wear such linen. I will take it to court."

So she went to the Tsar's palace and kept marching up and down in front of the windows. The Tsar saw her and asked: "What do you want, old dame?"

"Your majesty," she replied, "I have brought you some wonderful cloth. I do not want to show it to anyone except yourself."

The Tsar commanded that it be brought before him, and when he saw the linen he was dumfounded.

"What will you take for this?" he asked.

"It will not cost you anything, Tsar-father! I have brought it to you for a gift."

The Tsar thanked her and sent her off with handsome presents.

From that linen they started to make the Tsar some shirts. They cut them out, but they could not find a seamstress anywhere to make them. They searched long, and at last the Tsar summoned the old dame and said to her: "You were clever enough to spin and weave this cloth, you must be clever enough to make some shirts out of it."

"Sovereign, it was not I who spun and wove this cloth," said the old dame; "it is the work of my adopted daughter."

"Well, let her make them," he said.

The woman went home and told Vasilisa all about this.

"I knew," said Vasilisa, "that this work of my hands would not suit them."

She shut herself in her room and took hold of the work. She sewed steadily without once letting it out of her hands, and soon a dozen shirts were ready.

The dame took the shirts to the Tsar and Vasilisa washed her face and hands, combed her hair, dressed herself, and sat down at the window, waiting to see what would happen. Presently one of the Tsar's servants came into the old dame's yard and said: "Our sovereign Tsar wishes to see the clever artist who has made him the shirts and to reward her from his own hands."

Vasilisa went and showed herself before the eyes of the Tsar. When he saw the fair young girl he fell passionately in love with her. "No!" he exclaimed, "I will never part with you: you shall be my wife." So the Tsar took Vasilisa by her white hands and caused her to sit by his side, and so they celebrated a great wedding. Vasilisa's father soon afterwards returned home. He was delighted with her good fortune, and from that time forth he lived at his daughter's. Vasilisa took the old dame also to be with her; but the Doll she kept in her pocket to the very end of her days.

THE BRIGHT-HAWK'S FEATHER

NCE upon a time there lived an old man and his old wife, and they had three daughters. The oldest and the next oldest were gay girls, but the youngest was occupied only with the housework, and yet she was so beautiful that no tongue could describe or pen depict her. When she walked along the street every eye was fastened upon her; all the other girls were not to be compared with her.

One day the old man was getting ready to go to town to attend the fair, and he asked his daughters what he should buy for them.

The eldest said: "Buy me a coat."

And the next oldest said the same. "But what shall I get for you, my dear little daughter?" asked the old man of the youngest.

"Dear papa, buy me a ruby-red flower."

The old man began to laugh at his youngest daughter. "Well now, what do you want a ruby-red flower for, you stupid little girl? What good is there in that? I would rather buy you some nice piece of finery."

But in spite of all he said he could not change her mind.

"Buy me a ruby-red flower"—and that was the end of it.

The father bade them good-bye, got into his cart, and rode off to the city to the fair, where he bought his two older daughters what they asked him to get for them; but nowhere could he find the ruby-red flower, though he went through the whole fair from one end to the other; no such flower was to be found anywhere at all.

The old man drove home and he delighted the eldest daughter and the next older with their fine coats.

"Here, my dear daughters, are what you wanted me to get for you," said he; "but," turning to the youngest, "I could n't find any ruby-red flower for you."

"Very well," said she; "perhaps next time you will have better luck in finding it."

The two older sisters cut and sewed their new coats, and they made fun of their youngest sister.

"Oh, you stupid girl! What did you expect? You should have asked for something else!"

But of course she endured their gibes without saying a word.

Another time the father prepared to go to town again for the fair, and he asked: "Well, my daughters, what shall I get for you?"

The eldest asked for a new dress, and so did the middle one, but the youngest again said: "Buy me a ruby-red flower, papa dear."

The father bade them good-bye, took his seat in his cart, and drove off to town. He bought two dresses, but no sign of a ruby-red flower could his eyes behold.

When he got home he said, "Alas, my dear daughter, again I have had no luck in finding your ruby-red flower."

"No matter, dear father, perhaps another time you will have better luck."

Well then, a third time the old man made ready to go to town to the fair, and he said: "Tell me, my dear daughters, what I shall get for you."

The two older ones said: "Buy us some ear-rings, father dear."

But again the youngest repeated her "Buy me the ruby-red flower, father."

The old man bade them good-bye, took his seat, and drove off. He bought some gold ear-rings;

then he set to work to find the flower. He searched and searched, but nothing of the sort was to be found. He felt disappointed, and started to go home. He had hardly passed the city gate when he met by chance a very old, old man who carried in his hand a ruby-red flower.

"My dear little old man, sell me your ruby-red flower," he said.

"It is not for sale, it is a keepsake," replied the stranger; "but if you will let your youngest daughter marry my son, Finist the Bright-Hawk, then I will let you have the ruby-red flower for nothing."

The father thought the matter over in his mind.

"If I don't get the flower my dear little daughter will be bitterly disappointed, but if I take it I shall have to give her in marriage, and God knows who her husband will be."

He thought it over and he thought it over, but finally he decided to take the ruby-red flower.

"After all, what is the harm?" he asked himself. "Even after they are engaged, if it does not look well, we can break it off."

He drove home, gave his two oldest daughters their ear-rings, and to the youngest he handed the little flower, saying: "I do not like your little flower, my darling daughter, I do not like it at all." And he whispered softly in her ear: "You see, this little flower was a keepsake; I got it of a stranger, a little old man, on condition that I would let you marry his son Finist the Bright-Hawk."

"Do not be troubled, father dear," said his daughter in reply; "you see he is such a fine and courteous young man, and he flies like a bright hawk through the sky, but as soon as he touches the moist earth he becomes a fine young man again."

"So you know him, then?"

"I know him, yes, I know him, my dear father. Last Sunday he was at mass, and he kept gazing at me and I talked with him. You see he loves me, father dear."

The old man shook his head, looked at his daughter so pitifully, crossed himself, and said: "Go to your little room, my darling daughter. It is time to go to bed. Morning is wiser than Evening. We will think it over."

So the girl went to her room and put the ruby-red flower in water; then she opened the window and gazed out into the blue distance.

From somewhere or other there suddenly flew before her Finist the Bright-Hawk-of-the-gaudy-feathers, and he flew straight into the window, and as soon as he touched the floor he became a fine young man. The girl was startled, but as soon as he began to talk with her it is impossible to tell how gay and happy she felt in her heart.

They talked till dawn, no one knows about what, but as soon as it began to grow light Finist the Bright-Hawk kissed her and said: "Every night when you set the ruby-red flower in the window I will come flying to you, my darling. And here is a feather from my wing; if ever you want any fine things, take the feather and wave it to the right, and in a twinkling anything that your heart desires will be at your service."

He kissed her again, changed into a bright hawk, and flew off into the dark forest.

The young girl followed her betrothed with her gaze, then closed the window and went to bed.

From that time forth, every night she stood the ruby-red flower in the open window, and the fine young man, Finist the Bright-Hawk, always came to her.

Once it was a Sunday. The bells began to ring in church. The two older sisters prepared to go to mass. They dressed themselves in their smart new dresses, they put on new kerchiefs, they adorned their ears with their gold ear-rings, and they ridiculed their youngest sister.

"Oh, you stupid creature!" they said. "What are you going to wear? You have n't anything new to put on! Stay at home with your red flower!"

But she replied: "That is all right, my dear sisters; do not worry yourselves about me, I will say my prayers at home."

The two older sisters arrayed themselves like gay birds and went to mass, but the youngest one sat down at her little window, all soiled and bedraggled, in her wretched old coat, and she looked down on the orthodox people as they were wending their ways to God's church. They all were dressed in their fine clothes, the men in new kaftans, and the women in holiday sarafans and bright-colored variegated kerchiefs.

The young girl waited awhile, then she took the colored feather, looked at it, and waved it to the right. Instantly, from somewhere, appeared before her a glass coach, drawn by stallions, and servants in gold livery, while for herself were fine raiment and all sorts of adornments of the costliest and brightest colored precious stones.

In a twinkling the beautiful girl dressed herself, took her seat in the carriage, and was whirled away to church. The congregation gazed at her and marvelled at her beauty. "She must be some queen come from the ends of the earth," said the people one to another.

As soon as the choir began to sing the "Holy, holy" she left the church, took her seat in the coach, and was whisked away home. The orthodox people hurried out to see which way she went, but no matter where they looked not a sign of her was to be seen.

But our beauty hurried back to her feather, and she waved it to the left, and in a twinkling the servants took off her clothes and the coach vanished from sight.

There she was, sitting as before, as if nothing had happened, and was looking out of her little window as the orthodox congregation scattered to their homes. Her sisters also came home.

"Well, sister," said they, "there was such a beautiful woman at mass to-day; such an one was never seen before; no tongue could describe or pen depict her beauty. It must be some queen come from foreign shores, so splendidly was she dressed, so magnificently decked out."

The same thing happened the second Sunday and the third. You see, the beautiful girl mystified the orthodox people and her sisters and her father and her mother. But one last time she started to undress and she forgot to take out of her braided hair a diamond brooch.

The older sisters came from church and began to tell their young sister about the beautiful queen; but when they looked at her they saw the diamond glittering so brilliantly in her braided hair!

"Now, sister, what is that on you?" the girls exclaimed. "Why, just such a brooch the queen wore on her head this day! Where did you get it?"

The beautiful girl groaned in spirit and ran off to her little room. There was no end of questions and conjectures and whisperings, but the youngest sister said not a word, but only smiled a quiet smile.

So now the older sisters began to keep an eye on her; and at night they would listen at the door of her little room, and one time they overheard her talking with Finist the Bright-Hawk, and when dawn came they saw with their own eyes how he flew out of her window and hid behind the dark forest.

These girls, it seems, were wicked — the older sisters. They agreed together to put hidden knives in the window of their sister's little room so that the Bright-Hawk's gaudy wings might be clipped off on them. What they plotted they performed, and the youngest sister had not a suspicion of it. As usual, she set her ruby-red flower in the window, lay down on the bed, and fell sound asleep.

In the night the Bright-Hawk came flying up; he flapped his wings and flapped his wings, but he could not get into the chamber; all he did was to cut his wings. "Good-bye, lovely girl," he cried; "if you want to find me, then seek for me beyond the thrice-nine lands in the thirtieth kingdom. But before you find me you will wear out three pairs of iron shoes, you will break three iron staves, you will eat three iron wafers. Farewell, dear good girl!"

All this time the girl was asleep, but she seemed to hear through her dream the harsh words, and she tried to wake up but she could not.

In the morning she awoke and looked all around her. It was already bright day, but no sign of the fine young man! But when she looked at the window, there, criss-cross, stuck sharp knives, and from them, on the ruby-red flower, blood was dropping.

Long did the girl weep bitter tears, many sleepless nights did she sit by the window of her little room, again and again did she wave the gaudy feather, but all in vain — Finist the Bright-Hawk came no more flying to her, neither did any servants come.

At last, with tears in her eyes, she went to her father and asked him for his blessing.

"I am going," she said, "whither eyes look."

She ordered three pairs of iron shoes to be forged for her, three iron staves, and three iron wafers. With a pair of shoes on her feet and a staff in her hand, she started off in the direction from which the Bright-Hawk had come flying to her.

She entered the dim forest; she stumbled over stump and hump; already her iron shoes were wearing out, her staff broken, her wafer eaten, but still the beautiful girl kept walking on and on, and the forest grew ever darker, ever denser.

Suddenly she saw standing before her a little hut on hens' legs, and it kept turning round and round.

The girl cried out: "Little hut, little hut, stand with your back to the forest and your front to me."

The hut turned round with its front to her. She went into the little hut, and there lay Baba Yaga the Witch from corner to corner, her lips in a ridge, her nose in the ceiling. "Fu! fu! fu!" she cried. "Hitherto no eye ever saw or ear ever heard of Russian spirit, but to-day Russian spirit is marching through the free world and strikes you in the eye and throws itself into your face! Where are you going, my pretty maid? Do you arrive from a doughty deed, or do you strive for a doughty deed?"

"Grannie," she answered, "the Bright-Hawk used to be with me, but my sisters did me an injury. I am now in search of him."

"You will have to go far, little one! You will have to go even to the thrice-nine lands. The Bright-Hawk is living in the thrice-ninth kingdom, in the thirtieth realm, and he is already betrothed to the Tsar's daughter."

Then Baba Yaga gave food and drink to the beautiful girl whom God had sent, and put her to bed; and in the morning as soon as day began to dawn she woke her up, gave her a precious gift—a silver distaff and a golden spindle—and said: "Now go to my next older sister, and God be with you; she will give you some good advice.

And here is my gift to you,—a silver distaff and a golden spindle. You will begin to spin the flax, and it will make a golden thread. Follow it, and when you come to the thrice-ninth empire, to the thirtieth kingdom, to the edge of the blue sea, the Bright-Hawk's bride will come down to walk along the beach. Then you must begin to spin, and she will want to buy my gift to you. But, my pretty maid, you must not sell it to her; only ask to look at the Bright-Hawk."

Then Baba Yaga took a little ball, rolled it along the path, and bade the young girl follow it.

"Wherever the little ball rolls," said she, "there must you make your way."

The young girl thanked the old dame and went in the direction the ball was rolling. Again she walked through the dim forest, ever farther and farther, and the forest grew ever darker and thicker, and the tops of the trees struck the sky. A long, long time she walked, and her second pair of iron shoes were worn out, her second staff was broken, and she had devoured her second iron wafer; and at last the little ball rolled up to a small hut. This small hut stood, like the other, on hens' legs, and kept turning and turning.

The beautiful girl cried: "Little hut, little hut, stand with your back to the forest and with your front toward me! I want to go in and get something to eat."

The hut obeyed her; it turned its back to the forest and its front to the girl.

She entered, and there in the hut on the stove on the thrice-ninth brick lay Baba Yaga the Bony-leg, with her lips in a ridge and her nose through the ceiling.

"Fu! fu! fu!" she cried. "Hitherto no eye ever saw or ear ever heard of Russian spirit, but to-day Russian spirit is marching through the free world and strikes you in the eye and throws itself into your face! Where are you going, my pretty maid? Do you arrive from a doughty deed, or do you strive for a doughty deed?"

The maiden replied: "Grannie, the Bright-Hawk used to be with me, but my sisters did me an injury. I am now in search of him."

"Alas! my girl, my girl, your Finist is going to be married. This very day the wedding takes place!" exclaimed the Baba Yaga. She gave the beautiful girl food and drink and put her to bed, and the next morning, ere the dear sun had risen, she woke her up and gave her a costly gift — a silver dish and a golden egg — and she said to her: "Now go to my oldest sister, and God be with you; she will give you some good advice. And here is my gift to you — a silver dish and a golden egg. When you reach the thrice-ninth empire, the thirtieth kingdom, on the shores of the blue sea you will find the Bright-Hawk's bride walking on the beach, and you must remember to roll the egg on the plate. She will want to buy my gift of you, but, my pretty maid, don't you accept anything; only ask to look at the Bright-Hawk-of-the-gaudy-feathers."

The girl thanked the old dame, sighed, and again started after the little ball; and again she walked through the dim forest, on and on, and the forest grew ever darker and denser, and the tree-tops leaned against the sky. A long, long time she walked, and her third pair of iron shoes began to wear out and her third staff was broken, and her last iron wafer devoured. But at last the little ball rolled up to a small hut which, like the others, stood on hens' legs and kept on turning and turning.

The girl said to the hut: "Little hut, little hut, turn your back to the forest and your front to me! I want to go in and get something to eat."

The hut obeyed, and turned its back to the forest and its front to the beautiful girl.

In the hut was the Baba Yaga again, and she was the very oldest of the three.

"Fu! fu! fu!" she cried. "Hitherto no eye ever saw or ear ever heard of Russian spirit, but to-day Russian spirit is marching through the free world, and strikes you in the eye and throws itself into your face! Where are you going, my pretty maid? Do you arrive from a doughty deed, or do you strive for a doughty deed?"

The beautiful girl replied: "Grannie, the Bright-Hawk used to be with me, but my sisters did me an injury. He flew from me beyond the distant seas, beyond the lofty mountains, into the thrice-ninth empire, into the thirtieth kingdom; and now I am in search of him."

"Alas! my girl, my dear little girl! He is already married to the Tsar's daughter!" exclaimed Baba Yaga; and she gave her food and drink and put her to bed. In the morning, before the stars in the sky had put out their candles, she woke her up, gave her a costly gift—a gold embroidery-frame and needle—and said to her:

"Well, now go, my dear girl, and God with you and do not dally. Here is my gift to you—a gold embroidery-frame and needle. Only keep the needle and it will sew of itself. When you reach the thrice-ninth empire, the thirtieth kingdom, and come to the blue sea, the Tsar's daughter will come to you, and she will want to buy the embroidery-frame and the needle; but, my pretty one, accept nothing in return. Only ask to have a look at the Bright-Hawk."

The young girl thanked the old dame, wept bitterly, but started off after the little ball. And now the forest began to grow thinner and thinner. Presently the blue sea, wide and free, spread out before her; and yonder, far, far away, glittering like fire, flamed golden towers on lofty marble palaces.

"That must be Finist the Bright-Hawk's empire," said the maiden to herself, and she sat down on the damp sea-sand, took out her silver distaff and her golden spindle and began to spin, and the golden thread was formed.

Soon there came along the beach the Tsar's daughter with her maidens, and when she saw the beautiful girl she stopped short and wanted to buy the silver distaff and the golden spindle.

"Only let me look at the Bright-Hawk, princess dear, and I will let you have them for nothing," replied the girl.

"Well, the Bright-Hawk is asleep now and has forbidden anyone to disturb him. However, give me your silver distaff and golden spindle and I will let you see him!"

The Tsar's daughter took the distaff and the golden spindle, hastened back to the palace, thrust into the Bright-Hawk's cloak an enchanted brooch, so that he might sleep more soundly and not wake from his sleep for a long, long time, and then she ordered the serving-women to bring the beautiful girl into the palace to see the Bright-Hawk, while she herself went out to walk.

Long the maiden beat her breast, long did she weep over her dear love.

"Awake, awake, my darling Finist, my Bright-Hawk!" she cried. "Your chosen maiden has come to you. I have broken three iron staves, I have worn out three pairs of iron shoes, I have devoured three iron wafers, and all this time I have been searching for you, my darling."

But Finist slept on and could not wake up.

The Tsar's daughter having walked as long as she wanted to, came home. She drove the girl away and took out the magic brooch.

Then the Bright-Hawk awoke.

"Uh! how long I have slept!" said he.

"Someone was here and was weeping and lamenting over me; but I could not open my eyes, they were so heavy!"

"It was only a dream," replied the Tsar's daughter; "no one has been here."

The next day the beautiful girl again sat on the shore of the blue sea and rolled the golden egg on the silver plate.

The Tsar's daughter came out to take a walk, saw it, and said: "Sell it to me."

"Only let me look at the Bright-Hawk and I will let you have it for nothing."

The Tsar's daughter consented, and again stuck the magic brooch into the Bright-Hawk's cloak.

Again the beautiful girl wept bitterly over her dear love, but she could not waken him.

"Awake, awake, my bright Prince! It is I, your chosen maiden. I have come to you; I have broken three iron staves, I have worn out three pairs of iron shoes, I have eaten three iron cakes, and all this time I have been searching for you, my darling."

But the Bright-Hawk slept on and could not wake up.

The Tsar's daughter having walked as long as she wanted to, returned home, drove the girl away, and took out the magic brooch.

"Uh! how long I have slept!" said the Bright-Hawk, awaking and yawning. "Someone has been here and has been weeping and lamenting over me; but I could not open my eyes, they were so heavy."

"It was all a dream," replied the Tsar's daughter; "no one has been here."

On the third day the beautiful girl was sitting on the shore of the blue sea, depressed and sad, and she held in her hands the gold embroidery-frame, and the golden needle was embroidering by itself.

The Tsar's daughter saw it and wanted to buy it.

"Only let me look at the Bright-Hawk," replied the girl, "and I will give it to you."

The Tsar's daughter consented, hastened to the palace, and said: "Finist the Bright-Hawk, let me brush your hair."

She sat down to brush his hair, and she fastened into it the magic brooch.

Immediately he fell into a deep sleep. Then she sent her serving-women to get the beautiful girl.

She came and tried to wake her loved one; she threw her arms around him, she kissed him, and she wept all the time so bitterly. But no, he would not wake up. Then she began to smooth his hair and she loosened the magic brooch.

Instantly the Bright-Hawk woke up and saw the beautiful girl. How glad he was!

She told him the whole story as it had happened: how her wicked sisters had spied on her, how she had taken the long journey, and how she had traded with the princess.

He fell more deeply in love with her than before, kissed her lips, and without delay commanded all his nobles and princes and all the ranks of the people to assemble.

And he began to ask them: "How would you decide? With which wife must I spend my life—with the one that sold me or with the one that bought me?"

All the nobles and all the princes and all the ranks of the people decided with one voice: "Take the one that bought you!"

And this was what Finist-the-Bright-Hawk-of-the-gaudy-feathers did. And so they were married and they banqueted for three days and three nights.

I also was at that wedding, and I drank the mead; and if you don't believe it you may long for it, but you won't get a taste of it. They put a nightcap on me— Now what's the use of talking? I think I'll be off!

IVAN AND THE GRAY WOLF

NCE upon a time, in a certain kingdom, in a certain realm, lived a Tsar named Vuislaf. He had three sons of princely birth: the first was Prince Dimitri, the second Prince Vasili, and the third was Prince Ivan. This Tsar had a garden so rich that there was none like it in any country, and in this garden grew all kinds of precious trees that bore fruit and did not bear fruit; and the Tsar had one favourite apple-tree which bore nothing but golden apples. Now the Magic Bird was in the habit of flying into the Tsar's garden, and this bird had golden feathers and eyes like Oriental crystal. It used to fly into the garden every night and sit on the Tsar's favourite apple-tree and strip it of the golden apples and then fly away again.

The Tsar became greatly distressed on account of his apple-tree; therefore he summoned his three sons and said to them: "My beloved children! Which of you is able to catch the Magic Bird in my garden? To the one who will capture him alive I will give the half of my realm while I am still alive, and all of it after I am dead."

Then his sons cried with one voice: "Beloved sovereign and father, we will, with the greatest delight, try to capture the Magic Bird alive."

The first night Prince Dimitri went into the garden to watch; and taking his seat under the very apple-tree from which the Magic Bird robbed the apples, he fell asleep and did not hear a sound when the bird came flying over and took a great quantity of the fruit.

In the morning the Tsar summoned his son, Prince Dimitri, and asked him: "Well, my son, did you see the Magic Bird or not?"

He replied to his father: "No, my beloved sovereign and father, it did not make its appearance last night."

The next night Prince Vasili went into the garden to watch for the Magic Bird. He took his seat under the same apple-tree, and after he sat there an hour, and then another hour of the night, he fell so sound asleep that he did not hear the Magic Bird come flying over to strip off the apples.

In the morning the Tsar called him into his

presence and asked him: "Well, my beloved son, did you see the Magic Bird or not?"

"My dear sovereign and father," he answered, "it did not make its appearance last night."

On the third night Prince Ivan went into the garden to watch, and he took his place under the same apple-tree. He sat there an hour, then a second and then a third, and suddenly the whole garden was lighted up as if it had been illuminated with a multitude of bonfires. It was the Magic Bird, which came flying over and lighted on the apple-tree and began to steal the apples.

Prince Ivan crept up to it so stealthily that he was able to seize it by the tail. He could not hold it, however, and all that was left in his hand was one tail feather.

In the morning the Tsar had hardly awakened from his sleep ere Prince Ivan came to him and gave him the pretty feather. The Tsar was mightily glad that his youngest son had succeeded even in obtaining one feather from the Magic Bird. This feather was so wonderful and bright that if it were taken into a dark room it lighted it up as if it had been the red sun.

The Tsar put this feather into his cabinet as a thing that ought to be preserved forever. From that time forth the Magic Bird came no more into the garden.

Then the Tsar again summoned his three sons and said to them: "My dearly beloved children, go forth with my paternal blessing and capture the Magic Bird and bring it to me alive, and what I promised before shall be given to the one who brings the bird to me."

Prince Dimitri and Prince Vasili had conceived a bitter hatred against their youngest brother, Prince Ivan, because he had succeeded in getting a feather from the Magic Bird's tail. They received their father's blessing and went forth together to hunt for the bird. Then Prince Ivan also began to ask his father for his blessing. However much the Tsar strove to detain Ivan he could not help letting him go, because he was so urgent in his beseeching. So the young man got his father's blessing, chose a horse for himself, and started on his journey, not knowing at all what way it would take him.

As he rode along, far and near, high and low—and so quickly that it is more easily said than done—he came at last to a bare field, to green meadows. And in the bare field stood a stone monument, and on the monument were inscribed these words:

WHOEVER COMES STRAIGHT UP TO THIS MONUMENT
WILL BE COLD AND HUNGRY
WHOEVER COMES UP TO THE RIGHT SIDE
WILL HAVE HEALTH AND WEALTH
BUT HIS HORSE WILL DIE
AND WHOEVER COMES UP TO THE LEFT SIDE
WILL BE HIMSELF KILLED
BUT HIS HORSE WILL BE LEFT ALIVE AND WELL.

Prince Ivan read this inscription and went up to the monument by the right side, having this in his mind: that though his horse would be killed, still he himself would be left alive.

At first nothing happened, and he rode on one day, two days, three days, when suddenly there came running up to meet him an enormous Gray Wolf, who said: "Oho, young man, Prince Ivan, did n't you read what was inscribed on the monument?—that your horse would be killed? Why then did you come this way?"

The Gray Wolf uttered these words, then he tore Prince Ivan's horse in two and went off to one side.

Prince Ivan wept bitterly for his horse, but he pushed ahead on foot. He walked a whole day and was unspeakably weary, and was just thinking about sitting down to rest, when suddenly the Gray Wolf overtook him and said to him:

"I am sorry for you, Prince Ivan, because you are so tired walking. Good! Get on my back, on the Gray Wolf's back, and tell me where you want to go and why!"

Ivan told the Gray Wolf where he wanted to go, and the Gray Wolf galloped off with him faster than the horse, and after some time, toward nightfall, he brought him to a stone wall not so very high, and there the Wolf stopped and said:

"Now, Prince Ivan, get down from my back, from the Gray Wolf's back, and climb over this stone wall. There on the other side of the stone wall is a garden, and in that garden sits the Magic Bird in a golden cage. You may take the bird, but do not touch the cage. If you do they will seize you instantly."

Prince Ivan climbed over the wall into the garden, and there he saw the Magic Bird in a golden cage, and he was greatly charmed by her. He took the bird out of the cage and started back, but then he recollected himself and said in his heart:

"Here I have taken the Magic Bird, but what have I got to put her in?"

So he returned on his steps; but hardly had he taken up the golden cage ere there was a sudden noise and commotion throughout the whole garden, because strings were attached to the golden cage. The guards instantly woke up and came running into the garden, and they seized Prince Ivan with the bird and carried him off to the Tsar, whose name was Dolmat.

Tsar Dolmat was to the last degree wroth with Prince Ivan and roared at him in a thunderous angry voice: "Young man, are n't you ashamed for being a thief? Now who are you, and of what country, and who is your father, and what is your name?"

Prince Ivan answered him, saying: "I am the son of Tsar Vuislaf, and they call me Ivan. Your Magic Bird used to fly every night into our garden and rob my dear father's favourite apple-tree of its golden apples, and so my father sent me off to capture the bird and bring her to him."

"Oho, young man, Prince Ivan," replied the Tsar Dolmat. "Do you think it was a pretty way to do as you did? If you had come to me, I would have given you the Magic Bird honourably. But now would n't it be well for me to send out and proclaim to all nations how dishonourably you have acted in my realm? However, go forth, Prince Ivan, if you would do me a service. If you will proceed to the thirtieth realm beyond the thrice-ninth kingdom and get Tsar Afron's gold-maned horse for me, then I will forgive you your crime, and I will present the Magic Bird to you as a great mark of honour."

Prince Ivan was very downcast and went from Tsar Dolmat to the Gray Wolf and told him all that Tsar Dolmat had said. "Oho, young man, Prince Ivan," replied the Gray Wolf, "why did you not heed my words and let the gold cage alone?"

"I am to blame before you!" said Prince Ivan to the Wolf.

"All right, be it so!" replied the Gray Wolf. "Sit on my back, on the Gray Wolf's back; I will take you where you have to go."

Prince Ivan got on the Gray Wolf's back, and the Wolf ran as fast as an arrow flies, and how long he ran one cannot tell; but at last he came by night to the realm of Tsar Afron. As they came up to the Tsar's white marble stables the Gray Wolf said to Prince Ivan:

"Make your way into these marble stables, Prince Ivan, and take the horse of the golden mane. But there is hanging on the wall a golden bridle: do not touch it, or you will get yourself into trouble."

Prince Ivan, making his way into the white marble stables, took the horse, and started to go away again; but he saw the golden bridle hanging on the wall, and it pleased him so much that he took it down from the nail. But no sooner had he touched it than there came a rumble and a commotion throughout all the stables, because strings were attached to that bridle.

The stableguards came running in, and they seized Prince Ivan and took him to Tsar Afron. In a rage Tsar Afron began to ply him with questions:

"Oho, you are a fine young man! Tell me from what country you come, and who is your father, and what is your name?"

To these questions Prince Ivan replied: "I am the son of the Tsar Vuislaf, and they call me Ivan!"

"Oho, young man, Prince Ivan," said Tsar Afron, "is this the deed of an honourable knight? If you had come to me, I would have given you the gold-maned horse with all honour. But now would it not be well for me to send out and proclaim to all nations what a dishonourable thing you have done in my realm? However, go forth, Prince Ivan, if you would do me service. Go to the thrice-ninth kingdom from here, to the thirtieth realm, and get for me Queen Helena the Beautiful, whom I have long loved with all my heart and all my soul, but cannot reach; then I will forgive you your crime and I will present you with the gold-maned horse and the golden bridle with all honour. But if you do not do me this service, then I will proclaim it abroad to all the nations that you are a dishonourable thief."

Prince Ivan went away from the palace and wept bitterly. He came to the Gray Wolf and told him what had happened to him.

"Oho, you are a fine young man, Prince Ivan!" exclaimed the Gray Wolf. "Why did you disobey my word and take the golden bridle?"

"I am to blame before you!" said Prince Ivan to the Wolf.

"Very good, so be it!" continued the Gray Wolf. "Mount on my back, on the Gray Wolf's back; I will take you where you want to go."

Prince Ivan mounted on the Gray Wolf's back, and the Wolf ran as swiftly as an arrow, and at last he came to the realm of Queen Helena the Beautiful, to the golden streamlet which bordered a magical garden; and the Gray Wolf said to Prince Ivan:

"Now, Prince Ivan, dismount from me, from the Gray Wolf, and go back along the same road and wait for me in the open field under the green oak."

Prince Ivan went back whither he was bidden. The Gray Wolf sat down near the golden streamlet and waited until Queen Helena the Beautiful came down to walk in her garden.

Toward evening, when the dear sun was beginning to drop very near to the west, Queen Helena the Beautiful came to walk in the garden with her maidens and nobles. When she came close to the very place where the Gray Wolf was sitting, behind the streamlet, the Gray Wolf suddenly sprang across the streamlet into the garden, and seizing Queen Helena the Beautiful, sprang back again and galloped off with her with all his might and main.

He galloped up to the open field, where Prince Ivan was waiting under the green oak, and said to him: "Prince Ivan, get on my back, on the Gray Wolf's back, as quickly as possible."

Prince Ivan mounted on his back, and the Gray Wolf carried them both to Tsar Afron's realm. The maidens and nobles of Queen Helena's court ran all about and sent out in pursuit of them, but none of all the messengers was able to overtake the Gray Wolf, and so they had to go back home.

Prince Ivan, as he sat on the Gray Wolf's back with the beautiful Queen Helena, fell over head and ears in love with her, and she with him, and when the Gray Wolf came galloping into Tsar Afron's realm the prince was utterly dejected and began to weep tearfully.

The Gray Wolf asked him: "What are you weeping about, Prince Ivan?"

And in reply Prince Ivan said to him: "My friend Gray Wolf, how can I help weeping and help feeling dejected? I have fallen over head and ears in love with the beautiful Queen Helena and now I must give her up to Tsar Afron in exchange for the gold-maned horse; and if I don't give her up to him, then Tsar Afron will proclaim me dishonourable to all the nations."

"I have served you greatly, Prince Ivan," said the Gray Wolf, "but I will serve you in this service also. Listen, Prince Ivan! I will take the form of the beautiful Queen Helena, and you must give me to Tsar Afron and take the gold-maned horse. He will regard me as the real queen. And when you have mounted the gold-maned horse and have gone far, far away, then I will ask Tsar Afron to go and take a walk in the open field. And as soon as he lets me go with the maidens and nobles of the court, and I am with them in the open field, then do you call me to mind and I will be with you again."

When the Gray Wolf had uttered this speech he knocked against the damp earth and was changed into the beautiful Queen Helena. Prince Ivan took the Gray Wolf and went to Tsar Afron's court, and he bade the beautiful Queen Helena herself to wait for him behind the city. When Prince Ivan came to Tsar Afron with the pretended Helena, the Tsar was perfectly delighted in his heart because he had come into possession of the treasure that he had been desiring so long, and he handed over to Prince Ivan the horse of the golden mane.

Prince Ivan mounted this horse and rode off outside the city. There he took Helena the Beautiful on with him and rode away, keeping to the road that led to the realm of Tsar Dolmat. The Gray Wolf lived with Tsar Afron one day, a second day, and then a third day, in the place of the beautiful Queen Helena; but on the fourth day she went to Tsar Afron and asked permission to go to walk in the open field in order to drive away the terrible homesickness that tormented her.

How loud did Tsar Afron swear: "Ah! my beautiful Queen Helena, I will do everything for you!" And immediately he commanded the maidens and all the nobles of his court to accompany the beautiful queen into the open field.

Meantime Prince Ivan had been on his way with the real Helena, and was talking with her, and he forgot all about the Gray Wolf, when suddenly he remembered: "Ah, where is my Gray Wolf?"

And instantly arriving from somewhere the Gray Wolf stood before Prince Ivan and said to him: "Mount me, Prince Ivan, mount the Gray Wolf, and let the beautiful queen ride on the gold-maned horse."

Prince Ivan mounted the Gray Wolf, and they rode together to Tsar Dolmat's realm. How long they rode no one knows, but when they reached that realm they stopped three miles from the city. Prince Ivan began to ask the Gray Wolf:

"Listen, my dear friend, Gray Wolf, you have done me many a service. Serve me in this last affair also. Could n't you turn into the gold-maned horse? Because it seems to me as if I could not part with this gold-maned horse!"

Suddenly the Gray Wolf struck the moist earth and turned into a gold-maned horse. Prince Ivan left the beautiful Queen Helena in a green meadow with the real horse, mounted the Gray Wolf, and rode to the palace, to Tsar Dolmat.

And as soon as he got there, Tsar Dolmat recognised Prince Ivan coming on the gold-maned horse. He immediately rushed out of his palace, met the prince in his wide court, kissed him on his mouth, took him by the right hand, and led him into his white marble palace.

Tsar Dolmat in return for such a pleasure ordered a great feast prepared, and they took their places at the oaken tables, at the checked linen tablecloth. They ate, drank, and made merry, and thus feasted for two days, and on the third day Tsar Dolmat rewarded Prince Ivan with the Magic Bird and the golden cage.

The prince took the Magic Bird, went out of the city, sat on the gold-maned horse, together with the beautiful Queen Helena, and rode toward his own fatherland. Now Tsar Dolmat, on the following day, determined to ride his gold-maned horse in the open field, and he had hardly spurred up the horse when it threw him, and again becoming the Gray Wolf galloped off and overtook Prince Ivan.

"Prince Ivan!" he cried. "Mount me, the Gray Wolf, and let the beautiful Queen Helena ride on the gold-maned horse."

Prince Ivan mounted the Gray Wolf, and they proceeded on their way. As soon as the Gray Wolf had brought Prince Ivan to the place where he had torn the horse to pieces he stopped and said:

"Now, Prince Ivan, I have served you with ample faith and truth. Here in this place I tore your horse in two, and I have brought you back to this very place. Dismount from me, from the Gray Wolf. Now you have a gold-maned horse and I will no longer be your servant."

The Gray Wolf spoke these words and galloped off to one side, and Prince Ivan wept bitterly at parting with the Gray Wolf, but he rode on his way with the beautiful queen. How long he rode with Helena on the gold-maned horse it were hard to say, but when he came within twenty miles of his own realm, he stopped, dismounted, and sat down with the beautiful queen to rest under a tree. He fastened the gold-maned horse to the same tree, and set the cage and the Magic Bird in its golden cage and the golden bridle near him. And as they rested on the soft turf and talked together they fell asleep; and just at that time Prince Ivan's brothers, Prince Dimitri and Prince Vasili, coming from different lands, and without having succeeded in finding the Magic Bird, happened to be returning to their fatherland empty-handed. And by chance they came upon their brother Prince Ivan asleep. When they caught sight of the gold-maned horse on the turf and the Magic Bird in its golden cage, they were covetous of them, and they conceived the idea of killing their brother. Prince Dimitri unsheathed his sword and ran it through Prince Ivan. Then he aroused the beautiful Queen Helena and began to ply her with questions.

"Beautiful girl! from what country do you come and who is your father, and what is your name?"

The beautiful queen, seeing Ivan lying dead, was terribly frightened, and amid bitter tears replied:

"I am Queen Helena. Prince Ivan, whom ye have done to a cruel death, came and got me. Ye would have been good brothers-in-law if ye had come with him into the open field, and beaten him in fair fight; but now ye have killed him while he was asleep, and what advantage will ye receive from such a deed?"

At this Prince Dimitri pointed his sword at the beautiful Queen Helena's heart and said to her:

"Listen, Helena! You are now in our hands; we are going to take you to our sire, Tsar Vuislaf, and see to it that you tell him that it was we who got you and the Magic Bird and the gold-maned horse. If you fail to tell him this, we shall instantly put you to death!"

Helena, frightened out of her wits, agreed to this, and promised that she would say what they bade her say.

Then Prince Dimitri and Prince Vasili began to draw lots for the beautiful Queen Helena and the gold-maned horse. And according to the lot the queen fell to Prince Vasili, and the gold-maned horse to Prince Dimitri; and away they went to the city.

Prince Ivan lay dead in that place for thirty days, and at the end of that time the Gray Wolf came running up to him and recognised by the scent that it was Prince Ivan. He wanted to bring him to life again, but he did not know how to do it. Just then the Gray Wolf saw an old raven and two young ones flying over the body, and they were about to alight and devour Prince Ivan's flesh.

The Gray Wolf sprang behind a bush, and as soon as the young ravens had alighted on the ground and began to peck at Prince Ivan's body, he leaped out, seized one of the young ravens, and was going to tear it to pieces.

Then the old raven flew down to the ground, lighted not far from the Gray Wolf, and said to him: "Oho there, you Gray Wolf! Do not touch my little birdling; he has never done anything to you."

"Listen, then, Raven!" replied the Gray Wolf. "I will not touch your little birdling if you will serve me in a service. Fly away beyond the thrice-nine lands, to the thirtieth kingdom, and bring me the Water of Life and the Water of Death."

At this the raven said to the Gray Wolf: "I will serve you in this matter, only don't touch my son!"

These words said the raven, and flew away.

On the third day he came flying back and with him he brought two vials; in one the Water of Life, and in the other the Water of Death, and he gave the vials to the Gray Wolf. The Gray Wolf took the vials, tore the little raven to pieces, sprinkled it with the Water of Death and instantly the young raven grew together again; he sprinkled it with the Water of Life, the little raven spread its wings and flew off.

Then the Gray Wolf sprinkled the Water of Death over Prince Ivan; his dead body grew whole again. He sprinkled him with the Water of Life; Prince Ivan got to his feet and demanded: "Have I been asleep long?"

In reply the Gray Wolf said to him: "Yes, Prince Ivan, you would have slept an eternity if it had not been for me. You see your brothers killed you, and took for themselves the beautiful Queen Helena and the gold-maned horse and the Magic Bird. Now make haste as quickly as possible to your home. Your brother Vasili is going to marry your bride to-day—the beautiful Queen Helena. And in order that you may get there as quickly as possible, you had better mount me—mount the Gray Wolf; I will take you home."

Prince Ivan mounted, the Gray Wolf galloped with him to the realm of the Tsar Vuislaf, and after he had been a long or short time on the way he took him to the city. Prince Ivan dismounted from the Gray Wolf, hurried into the city, and going to the palace he learned that his brother Prince Vasili had returned with the queen from the wedding ceremony and was sitting at table.

Then Helena the beautiful caught sight of

Prince Ivan and instantly sprang from the table and began to kiss his lips crying:

"This is my darling husband, Prince Ivan, and not that wicked wretch who is sitting at table!"

Then the Tsar got up from his place and began to question her as to the meaning of all this. And Helena told him all the truth in regard to what had taken place.

Tsar Vuislaf was bitterly indignant with Prince Dimitri and Prince Vasili, and sent them to jail. But Prince Ivan married the beautiful Queen Helena, and lived with her so lovingly that neither one could endure to exist a single instant without the other.

THE LITTLE SISTER AND LITTLE BROTHER

WO orphans, little Sister Aliona and little Brother Ivan, were walking across a wide field by a long path, and it was hot and the heat tortured them.

They went and they went and they went. The sun rode high and little Ivan grew thirsty.

"Sister Aliona, I want a drink," he said.

"Wait a while, brother, we shall come to a well," she answered.

The well was a long way off, the heat tortured them, and they reeked with perspiration. As they walked along they saw a pond, and around the pond a herd of cows was feeding.

"I want a drink," said little Ivan.

"Do not drink here, brother! If you do you will turn into a calf," said Aliona.

He heeded her and they went on. They walked and they walked and they saw a river, and near the river was a drove of horses.

"Oh, sister! If you only knew how thirsty I am!" he cried.

"Do not drink, brother! If you should, you would become a little colt," she answered.

Little Ivan obeyed her and they went on. They walked and they walked and they saw a lake, and around it was grazing a flock of sheep.

"Oh, sister! I am terribly thirsty!" he said again.

"Do not drink, brother! If you do you will turn into a lamb," she replied.

Again little Ivan heeded her and they went on. They walked and they walked and they saw a brook, and on its banks swine were rooting.

"Oh, sister!" he pleaded. "I must have a drink. I am terribly thirsty."

"Do not drink, brother! If you do you will become a pig."

Again little Ivan heeded what she said and they went on. They walked and they walked, and they saw a herd of goats grazing near some water.

"Oh, sister! I must have a drink!" he said earnestly.

"Do not drink, brother!" she besought. "If you do you will turn into a kid!"

But he could no longer restrain himself, and he disobeyed his sister. He took a drink and instantly was changed into a Kid, running and gambolling in front of his sister and crying, "Baa! baa!"

Aliona suspected that it was her brother. She sat down in the shade of a hayrick and burst into bitter tears, but the Kid ran about on the grass near her. She tied a silken scarf around him and led him along with her, and she wept, bitterly she wept.

The Kid ran and ran and finally ran into the garden of a certain Tsar. The men perceived it and immediately called the Tsar's attention to it.

"Your majesty," they said, "a Kid has just run into our garden, and a girl has him by a girdle, and she is such a beauty!"

The Tsar commanded to find out who she was. So the people went and asked her whence she came and what her name was.

"My name is so-and-so," said Aliona, "and I had a father and mother, but they died and only we children were left, I myself and this my brother little Ivan. We were coming a long way and we kept on walking and walking when we saw a herd of goats grazing near some water, and my brother could not restrain himself; he drank a little of the water and was changed into a Kid."

The men reported this to the Tsar. The Tsar summoned Aliona and asked her about everything. She was pleasing in his sight and he wanted to marry her.

"Come!" said he, "follow me. I will give you fine clothes and silver, and I will not neglect the Kid; wherever you are there he shall be also."

The wedding quickly took place and they began to live together, and the Kid with them. He used to disport himself in the garden, and eat and drink with the Tsar and Tsaritsa. Good men gazing at them were delighted, but evil-minded men were full of envy.

One time the Tsar went hunting, and while he was away a witch came and cast a spell on the Tsaritsa, so that she became ill, very weak, and pale.

At the Tsar's everything faded; in the garden the flowers began to wither; the trees dried up; the grass grew sear. The Tsar came home and asked the Tsaritsa: "Are you ill?"

"Yes, I am indisposed," replied the Tsaritsa.

The next day the Tsar went hunting again, but Aliona lay at home sick.

The witch came to her and said: "Would you like me to cure you? Go to a certain lake at dawn and drink the water there."

The Tsaritsa heeded her, and in the early morning she went to the lake, but the witch was there waiting for her and seized her, hung a stone around her neck, and flung her into the water. Aliona went to the bottom. The Kid came running down to the water and bitterly, bitterly lamented.

Then the witch took the shape of the Tsaritsa, arrayed herself in her fine clothes, and went to the palace.

The Tsar came home and was delighted because the Tsaritsa was restored to health again. They sat down to dinner and began to eat.

"But where is the Kid?" demanded the Tsar.

"We do not need him," replied the witch. "I would not let him come in, he smells so goaty."

The next day, as soon as the Tsar had gone off hunting, the witch began to beat the poor little Kid. She pounded him and pounded him, and said in threatening tones: "When the Tsar comes home I will ask him to have you killed."

The Tsar came and immediately the witch began to urge him: "Give your command, yes, give your command to kill the little Kid. He is a nuisance to me, he is entirely detestable to me!"

The Tsar felt sorry for the poor little Kid, but there was no help for it, she was so insistent, she was so urgent, that the Tsar at last consented for him to be killed.

The Kid saw how they were beginning to sharpen the steel knives for him; he lamented. He ran to the Tsar and besought him: "Tsar, let me go down to the lake and get a drink of water and bathe myself!"

The Tsar let him go. As soon as the poor little Kid reached the lake he stood on the shore and cried out piteously:

"Dear Aliona, sister mine!
Come forth, come forth upon the shore!
The flaming fire is burning bright,
The boiling pot is bubbling o'er,
They 're sharpening the steely knife,
They 're going to take away my life."

She replied to him:

"Oh, Ivan, little brother, dear!
A heavy stone keeps me down here,
A cruel snake gnaws at my heart."

The poor little Kid lamented and went back home. At noon he again asked the Tsar: "Tsar, let me go down to the lake and get a drink of water and bathe myself."

The Tsar let him go. The poor little Kid ran down to the lake again, and began to lament piteously:

> "Dear Aliona, sister mine!
> Come forth, come forth upon the shore!
> The flaming fire is burning bright,
> The boiling pot is bubbling o'er,
> They 're sharpening the steely knife,
> They 're going to take away my life."

She answered him:

> "Oh, Ivan, little brother dear!
> A heavy stone keeps me down here,
> A cruel snake gnaws at my heart."

The poor little Kid lamented and went home.

But the Tsar began to think: "What can this mean? The little Kid keeps going down to the lake."

Then for the third time the poor little Kid asked: "Tsar, let me go down to the lake and get a drink of water and bathe myself."

The Tsar let him go, but this time followed him.

Going down to the lake he listened as the Kid called to his sister:

"Dear Aliona, sister mine!
Come forth, come forth upon the shore!
The flaming fire is burning bright,
The boiling pot is bubbling o'er,
They 're sharpening the steely knife,
They 're going to take away my life."

And she replied:

"Oh, Ivan, little brother dear!
A heavy stone keeps me down here,
A cruel snake gnaws at my heart."

But now the poor little Kid began to call to his sister to come to the surface.

Aliona swam up to the top and showed herself above the water. The Tsar seized her, took the stone from her neck, and dragged her ashore, and then asked her how this had happened, and she told him the whole story. The Tsar was very glad, and so was the poor little Kid, and he gambolled about, and in the garden everything grew green and burst into bloom again.

The Tsar ordered the wicked witch to be punished. They gathered a pile of wood in the courtyard and burned her alive. And after this the Tsar and the Tsaritsa and the little Kid lived, and lived happily and lived well, and they ate and drank together just as they used to do before.

TRANSLATOR'S NOTE. — This story is plainly a nature myth. The wicked witch is Winter, who temporarily drives away the Summer or Spring, but when she returns the Tsar's garden blooms again and the little Kid gambols around the bountiful table. That explains why the Kid is not restored to his pristine form. He stands for the young life of the world in the early Spring.

THE WHITE DUCKLING

A CERTAIN prince took for his wife a very beautiful princess; but he had hardly time to look at her, hardly time to have a talk with her, hardly time to hear her speak, before he found it necessary for him to take leave of her, necessary for him to go on a long journey and to entrust his wife to the care of others. What help for it? One can't take forever in kissing and saying good-bye.

The princess wept many tears. The prince gave her much good advice, forbade her to leave her lofty enclosure, or to go into company, or to gossip with naughty people, or to listen to idle talk. The princess promised to obey him in all things. The prince went away. The princess locked herself in her room and did not leave it.

After some time a little woman came to her, apparently so simple-hearted, so friendly!

"What!" she exclaimed, "are you lonely? If you would only look out into God's world, if you would only go down into the garden it would banish all your melancholy, it would cool your head."

For a long time the princess argued against it. No, she would not do it. But at last she said to herself, "It is no sin to go down into the garden," and she went.

In the garden flowed crystal-clear spring water.

"Why!" exclaimed the little woman, "the day is so warm, the sun is scorching, but the water is icy cool. See how it dashes! Could n't we have a bath here?"

"No, no, I will not!" she replied. But at the same time she said to herself: "Why! there 's no sin in taking a bath."

So she stripped off her dress and jumped into the water. As soon as she had ducked under, the little woman gave her a tap on the back.

"Swim off," said she, "a little White Duckling." And immediately the princess swam away in the shape of a White Duckling.

Then the sorceress put on the princess's clothes and ornaments, painted her cheeks, and sat down to wait for the prince. As soon as the puppy barked and the bell jingled, she ran to meet the prince, threw herself into his arms, kissed him, and caressed him. He was so glad he clasped her in his arms and did not recognise the deception.

But the White Duckling laid some eggs, and hatched two little ones that were beautiful and a third that was ugly, and these little ones became children. She nurtured them and they began to run along by the brook, to catch the gold fish, to collect rags and to fashion coats, to play on the bank, and to look out on the pretty meadow.

"Oh, do not go there, children!" said the mother.

But the children did not heed her. To-day they played on the turf, to-morrow on the green grass. They kept venturing farther and farther, and so they made their way into the prince's yard. The wicked sorceress instantly recognised them, and she gnashed her teeth. She called the children to her, gave them something to eat and to drink, and put them to bed. Then she ordered a fire to be built, and the kettle to be hung over it, and knives to be sharpened.

The two pretty brothers lay down and slept, but the mother had told the ugly sister to come and lie against her breast so as not to catch cold. So the ugly one could not sleep, but kept her eyes wide open and her ears wide open.

In the night the wicked sorceress came to the door and asked: "Are you asleep, children, or are you awake?"

The ugly one replied: "Whether we are asleep or not, we have made up our minds that they are going to kill us all. The red-hot fire is built, the bubbling pot is hung, the steely knives are sharpened."

"They are not asleep," said the sorceress, and she went away.

After awhile she came back again to the door. "Are you asleep, children, or not?"

The ugly one made the same answer: "Whether we are asleep or not, we have made up our minds that they are going to kill us. The red-hot fire is built, the bubbling pot is hung, the steely knives are sharpened."

"Why is it always one voice replies?" wondered the sorceress. She opened the door a little way and perceived that the two brothers were sound asleep. Instantly she touched them with her deathly hand and they died.

In the morning the White Duckling called her children; they did not come. Her heart had a presentiment. She shook her wings and flew into the prince's courtyard. In the courtyard, white as napkins, cold as clods, lay the brothers side by side. She flew down to them, threw herself on them, spread her wings, pressed close to them, and in a mother's voice cried out:

"Krya! krya! my children sweet!
Krya! krya! my darling dears!
I nurtured you in sorrow deep,
I made you drink my bitter tears,
On darkest nights I did not sleep,
No morsel sweet I took to eat!"

"Wife! Do you hear this marvellous thing?" said the prince to the sorceress. "A duckling is talking!"

"What is wonderful about that?" scoffed the witch. "Order the duckling driven out of the yard."

They drove her out, but she flew back again to her children:

"Krya! krya! my children sweet!
Krya! krya! my darling dears!
A wicked witch has murdered you!
A wicked witch, a cruel snake,
A cruel snake, a viper too!
She robbed you of your loving sire,
Your loving sire, my heart's desire!
She sunk us in the rapid river,
She changed us into ducklings white,
But *she* lives on and boasts her might!"

"Aha!" said the prince to himself, and he cried out: "Bring me the White Duckling!"

All started off, but the White Duckling flew away and would not give herself up to anyone. Then the prince himself went in pursuit of her, and she fluttered down into his hands.

He took her under the wings, and she began to change into different reptiles. The prince was not alarmed; he did not let her out of his hands. After a time she changed into a spindle. The prince broke the spindle in two. One end he threw in front of him, the other end he threw behind him, and he said: "Let a white birch stand behind me, and a beautiful maiden in front of me!"

A white birch grew up behind him and a beautiful maiden stood in front of him, and in the beautiful maiden the prince recognised his young princess. When the princess perceived her children lying side by side, white as napkins, cold as clods, she burst into bitter tears:

"My children! O my darling dears!
I nurtured you in sorrow deep,
I made you drink my bitter tears!
A wicked witch has murdered you,
A wicked witch, a cruel snake,
A cruel snake, a viper too!"

When the prince looked at the princess he also wept. He ordered the sorceress to be brought out, and when she came he commanded her to bring the children to life again.

The sorceress was very angry, she gnashed her teeth, but she saw that there was no help for it. So she told them to catch a certain Raven and attach to it two vials, and order the Raven to bring in one the Water of Life and in the other the Water of Speech.

The raven flew away and brought back the water. They sprinkled the children with the Water of Life; they began to move. They sprinkled them with the Water of Speech; they spoke. And so the prince and his whole family from that time forth lived and flourished, and lived well and forgot what trouble had passed.

But they fastened the sorceress to a horse's tail, and she was torn to pieces over the field. Where a leg was torn off there lay a poker, and where an arm was torn off they found a rake, and where her head was torn off, there was a shrub and a stump. And the birds came and pecked it to pieces, and the winds blew the dust away, so that nothing was left of her — not a trace, nor even a memory!

MARYA MOREVNA

N a certain kingdom, in a certain realm, once lived Prince Ivan and his three sisters. One was Princess Marya, the second was Princess Olga, and the third was Princess Anna. Their father and mother were dead. When they were dying they gave this command to their son:

"Whoever comes wooing your sisters first, let them have them. Don't keep them long in your house!"

The prince buried his parents, and full of grief went with his sisters to walk in the green garden. Suddenly a black cloud arose in the sky and a terrible storm came on them.

"Come, let us go into the house, sisters," exclaimed Prince Ivan.

They had hardly got indoors ere the thunder crashed, the ceiling cracked, and a bright Hawk flew down through it into the room where they were. As soon as the Hawk touched the floor, he turned into a fine young man who said:

"Your health, Prince Ivan. Hitherto I have been here as your guest, now I have come as a suitor. I should like to take your sister, the Princess Marya, as my wife."

"If my sister likes you I have no objection. Let her go with you under God's care."

The Princess Marya was willing; so the Hawk took her as his wife and carried her off to his kingdom.

Days followed days, hours trod on the heels of hours. Almost a whole year had passed. Prince Ivan and his two sisters went to stroll in their green garden. Again a cloud came up with a fierce wind, with lightning. "Come, sisters, let us go into the house!" said the prince.

They had hardly got indoors ere a thunderbolt struck the roof, which tumbled in, the ceiling split, and an Eagle flew down. As soon as the Eagle touched the floor it became a fine young man:

"Good day to you, Prince Ivan," he said. "Hitherto I have visited you as a guest, but now I have come as suitor."

And he asked for the hand of Princess Olga.

Prince Ivan replied:

"If you please Princess Olga, let her go with you; but I do not force her against her will."

Princess Olga consented and became the Eagle's wife. The Eagle caught her up and bore her away to his kingdom.

Still another year passed. Prince Ivan said to his youngest sister: "Come, let us walk in the green garden."

They had been strolling about a little while when again a cloud appeared with a fierce wind and with lightning.

"Come, sister, let us go home," he said.

They went into the house, and hardly had they sat down when there was a crash of thunder, the ceiling split, and a Raven flew down to them. As soon as the Raven touched the floor it turned into a fine young man. The other birds had been fine, but this was the finest of all.

"Well, Prince Ivan," he said, "hitherto I have come as a guest, but now I am here as a suitor. Give me Princess Anna."

"I do not control my sister's will; if you are in love with her, let her go with you."

Princess Anna followed the Raven and he took her to his realm. Prince Ivan remained alone. A whole year he lived without his sisters, and his life became dull to him. Said he: "I am going to find my sisters."

He set out and he travelled and he travelled, and at last he saw before him a great army defeated. Prince Ivan asked: "If there is a man alive here let him answer. Who conquered this great host?"

A living man answered: "Marya Morevna, the beautiful queen, conquered this mighty host."

Prince Ivan proceeded on his way, and he came to white tents, and Marya Morevna, the beautiful queen, came to meet him.

"Your good health, prince," she said, "whither does God bring you — of your own will or against your own will?"

Prince Ivan replied: "Brave young men do not go against their own will."

"Well if your business does not demand haste, come and be my guest in my camp," she replied.

Prince Ivan was glad of that. He spent two nights in the queen's camp, and he fell in love with Marya Morevna and took her as his wife. Marya Morevna, the beautiful queen, took him with her to her kingdom, where they lived together for some time. Then it occurred to the queen to prepare for a war. She entrusted everything to Prince Ivan and gave him this injunction: "Go everywhere and look after everything; only it is forbidden you to look into this storeroom."

That was more than he could bear. As soon as Marya Morevna had gone, he rushed to the storeroom, opened the door, and looked around. And there hung Koshchei the Deathless,[1] fastened with twelve chains.

Koshchei besought Prince Ivan:

"Have pity upon me and give me a drink! For ten years have I been tormented here, and I have had nothing to eat or to drink and my throat is all dried up."

The prince gave him a whole bucket of water. He drank it down with one gulp and asked for more.

"One bucket is not enough to quench my thirst; give me some more!"

The prince gave him another bucket full. Koshchei drank it down also and asked for yet a third. As soon as he had drained the third he regained all his pristine strength, took the twelve chains, and broke them all at once.

"Thank you, Prince Ivan," said Koshchei the Deathless. "Now you will never see Marya Morevna again, no matter how you may long for her!" And with a terrible whirlwind he flew out of the window, fell upon Marya Morevna, the beautiful queen, on the way, seized her, and carried her off.

---

[1] Personification of Death.

Now Prince Ivan wept bitterly, and started down the road.

"Whatever happens I will go and find Marya Morevna," he said.

He went one day, he went two days, and at dawn of the third he saw a wonderful palace, and near the palace stood an oak-tree, and on the oak-tree sat a bright Hawk. The Hawk flew down from the oak-tree and as soon as he lighted on the ground he turned into a fine young man and cried out:

"Ah, my beloved brother-in-law! I hope the Lord is good to you!"

The Princess Marya came running out, and she joyously welcomed Prince Ivan, and began to ask him about his health, and to tell him all about her manner of life.

The prince stayed with them three days, and then said: "I cannot stay any longer with you; I am going in search of my wife, Marya Morevna, the beautiful queen."

"It will be hard for you to find her," said the Hawk. "Leave here your silver spoon at all events; we shall be able to look at it and remember you by it."

Prince Ivan left his silver spoon with the Hawk and went on his way. He went one day, went two days, and at dawn of the third day he saw a palace still finer than the first, and near the palace stood an oak-tree, and on the oak-tree sat an Eagle. The Eagle flew down from the oak-tree, and as soon as it touched the ground it turned into a fine young man who cried out: "Make haste, Princess Olga, our dear brother is coming!"

The Princess Olga came running out to meet him, began to hug him and kiss him, asked after his health, and told him all about her manner of life.

Prince Ivan visited with them three short days, and then said: "I cannot stay any longer; I am going to find my wife, Marya Morevna, the beautiful queen."

The Eagle replied: "It will be hard for you to find her. Leave with us your silver fork; when we look at it we shall have something to remember you by."

He left them his silver fork and started on his way. He went one day, he went a second day, and at dawn of the third day he saw a palace still better than the first two, and near the palace grew an oak-tree, and on the oak-tree sat a Raven. The Raven flew down from the oak-tree, and as soon as he touched foot to the ground he turned into a fine young man who cried out: "Princess Anna, come quickly, here is our brother!"

Princess Anna came running out, met him joyously, began to hug him and kiss him, and asked after his health, and told him all about her manner of life.

Prince Ivan visited with them three short days, and then he said: "Good-bye, I am going off to find my wife, Marya Morevna, the beautiful queen."

The Raven replied: "It will be hard for you to find her. Leave with us your little silver snuff-box; when we look at it we shall have something to remember you by."

The prince gave him his little silver snuff-box, said good-bye, and started on his way. He went one day, and he went a second day, but on the third day he found Marya Morevna. When she saw her husband she threw herself on his neck and burst into tears exclaiming:

"Oh, Prince Ivan, why did you not heed me? Why did you look into the storeroom and let Koshchei the Deathless escape?"

"Forgive me, Marya Morevna! Do not recall what is past and gone. Come, let us go away together, since Koshchei is not in sight. Perhaps he will not overtake us."

So they got their things and started off.

Now Koshchei was out hunting, but toward evening he returned home. His good steed stumbled under him.

"What is the matter with you, you hungry jade? What makes you stumble? Do you scent some misfortune?"

The horse replied: "Prince Ivan has come and carried off Marya Morevna."

"But we can overtake them, can't we?"

"One may sow wheat and wait till it grows, till it is harvested, till it is ground, till it is made into flour, till it is baked into five loaves of bread, and all that time you would be in pursuit of them. But if we are going to try, it is time to start."

Koshchei galloped away and overtook Prince Ivan.

"Now look here," said he, "I will forgive you this once on account of your kindness to me in giving me a drink of water, and a second time I will forgive you; but the third time beware. I will chop you up into mincemeat!"

He seized Marya Morevna and carried her off, and Prince Ivan sat down on a stone and wept. He wept and wept and started off again in search of Marya Morevna. When he at last found her again, it happened that Koshchei the Deathless was not at home.

"Let us go, Marya Morevna!" he said.

"Oh, Prince Ivan, he will overtake us!" she replied.

"Let him overtake us then. At any rate we shall have spent a sweet hour together."

They got ready and started off.

Koshchei the Deathless was on his way home, and his good horse stumbled under him.

"What is the matter with you, you hungry jade? What makes you stumble? or do you scent some misfortune?"

"Prince Ivan has come after Marya Morevna and has taken her off with him."

"Well, we can overtake them, can't we?"

"You can sow barley and wait till it has grown, till it is harvested, till it is ground, till it is brewed into beer, till it has made people drunk, and they have slept it off, before you will catch them. But if you are going to do it, we had better make haste."

Koshchei galloped away and overtook Prince Ivan.

"I told you once that you should never see Marya Morevna, no matter how much you might wish to!" he exclaimed.

Then he seized her and carried her off with him.

Prince Ivan was left alone. He wept and he wept, and again he started after Marya Morevna. This time also, by good luck, Koshchei was not at home. "Let us go, Marya Morevna!" he said.

"Oh, Prince Ivan," she exclaimed, trembling, "he will surely catch us, and he will hack you to pieces!"

"Let him hack me to pieces!" he replied fiercely, "I cannot live without you."

So they got ready and started off.

Koshchei the Deathless was on his way home, and his good steed stumbled under him. "Why do you stumble?" said he. "Do you scent some misfortune?"

"Prince Ivan has come after Marya Morevna and has carried her away," the steed answered.

Without loss of time Koshchei galloped after them, overtook Prince Ivan, and cut him into mincemeat, and put him into a pitchy cask. He took this cask, fastened it with iron hoops, and flung it into the blue sea; and he carried Marya Morevna off with him.

At this very time the silver articles that Prince Ivan had left at his brothers-in-law turned black. "Oh," they exclaimed, "some misfortune has evidently taken place!"

The Eagle dived down into the blue sea, seized the cask, and brought it up on shore. The Hawk flew off and brought the Water of Life. The Raven flew off and brought the Water of Death. All three settled down in one place, broke open the cask, took out the bits of Prince Ivan, washed them, and put them together as they belonged. The Raven sprinkled them with the Water of Death; the body grew together again, all in one piece. The Hawk sprinkled it with the Water of Life; Prince Ivan shuddered a little, got to his feet, and said: "Oh, how long I have been sleeping!"

"You would have slept much longer if it had not been for us," replied his brothers-in-law. "Now come and make us a visit."

"No, brothers, I am going to find Marya Morevna," he answered. So a fourth time he went on his quest, and when he found her he entreated her: "Find out from Koshchei the Deathless where he got such a good steed."

So Marya Morevna seized a favorable opportunity and began to ply Koshchei with questions. Koshchei said in reply:

"Beyond the thrice-nine kingdoms, in the thirtieth realm, beyond the fiery river, lives the Baba Yaga. She has such a mare, and on it every day she flies around the world. And she has many other splendid mares. I served her as a herdsman for three days, and as I did not let one single mare escape, the Baba Yaga gave me one little colt."

"How did you cross the fiery river?"

"Oh, I have such and such a handkerchief, and when I wave it three times toward the right it grows into a high, high bridge, and the fire cannot reach it."

Marya Morevna listened to what he said, and she told it all to Prince Ivan, and she got the handkerchief and gave it to him.

Prince Ivan managed to cross the fiery river, and he went to find the Baba Yaga. Long, long he travelled without eating or drinking. A strange bird happened to meet him with her little ones. Prince Ivan said: "I will eat one of her fledglings."

"Do not eat it, Prince Ivan," besought the strange bird; "sometime I may be able to help you."

He went on and on. In the forest he saw a hive of bees. Said he: "I guess I will take a little honey." The little bee-mother begged him not to. "Do not touch my honey, Prince Ivan! Sometime I may be able to help you."

He refrained from touching it, and went on his way, and happened to fall in with a lioness and her cub.

"I have a mind to eat this lioness; I'm so hungry that it makes me sick."

"Do not touch me, Prince Ivan," she entreated, "sometime I may be able to help you."

"Very good, just as you please."

He went on slowly, half-starved, and he went and he went, and at last there stood the Baba Yaga's house, and around the house were a dozen stakes, and on each of the dozen stakes except one was a man's skull.

"Good afternoon, grannie!" he said.

"Good afternoon, Prince Ivan! Why did you come—of your own good will or because you had to?"

"I came to serve you for a gallant horse."

"So be it, prince! You need not serve me for a whole year, but three days will be enough! If you guard my mares well, I will give you a gallant steed. But if not, do not be angry; your head will be stuck on the last of the stakes."

Prince Ivan agreed; the Baba Yaga gave him food and drink and bade him attend to his work.

As soon as he had driven the mares out into

the field, they began to switch their tails, and all of them darted in different directions across the meadows. The prince could not follow them with his eyes, so quickly did they disappear from sight. Then he wept and mourned, and he sat down on a stone and fell asleep. The dear sun was already setting when a strange bird flew up to him and awoke him.

"Wake up, Prince Ivan, the mares are at home now!" The prince got up, went home, and the Baba Yaga was making a clamor and shouting to her mares: "What have you come home for?"

"Why shouldn't we come home?" they answered. "Birds came flying from all over the world, and they almost pecked our eyes out."

"Well, then, see that to-morrow you don't go to the meadows, but scatter through the thick forest."

Prince Ivan slept all night, and in the morning the Baba Yaga said to him: "Look here, prince! If you do not watch the mares well, if a single one is lost, your proud head will adorn the stake."

He drove the mares out to pasture. Instantly they switched their tails and scattered through the thick forest.

Again the prince sat down on a stone and wept and wept and fell asleep. The dear sun was sinking behind the forest, when a lioness came running up to him, crying: "Prince Ivan, wake up! the mares are all stabled."

Prince Ivan woke up and went home. The Baba Yaga was scolding worse than before and shouting to her mares: "Why did you come home?"

"Why shouldn't we come home? Fierce wild beasts were running up from all parts of the world, and they almost tore us to pieces."

"Well, to-morrow drive them into the blue sea."

Again Prince Ivan slept all night, and in the morning the Baba Yaga commanded him to pasture her mares: "If you do not watch them well, your proud head will set on the stake!"

He drove the mares out to pasture, and instantly they switched their tails and ran down into the blue sea, and stood in the water up to their necks. Prince Ivan sat down on a stone and cried himself to sleep.

The dear sun was sinking behind the forest, when a bee came flying up to him and said:

"Prince, wake up! The mares are all stabled. But as soon as you go home, do not show yourself to the Baba Yaga. Go into the stable and hide behind the stalls. There you will find a scurvy colt. Steal him and in the deep dead of night leave the place."

Prince Ivan got up, went to the stable, and crept behind the stalls. The Baba Yaga was storming and crying to her mares: "Why did you return home?"

"Why shouldn't we return home? A swarm of bees flew from somewhere out of the whole world and stung us all about till the blood came."

The Baba Yaga went to sleep, and that very night Prince Ivan stole from her the scurvy colt, saddled him, mounted him, and galloped off to the fiery river. As soon as he reached the fiery river he waved the handkerchief three times to the right, and lo and behold! no one knows how, a lofty, splendid bridge arched the river. The prince crossed the bridge and waved the handkerchief only twice toward the left, and lo! a small slender bridge remained over the river.

In the morning the Baba Yaga woke up and she could not see her scurvy colt anywhere. She flew into a fury. With all her might and main she leaped into her iron mortar, whipped it up with her pestle, and swept away the tracks with her besom. She galloped up to the fiery river, looked at it, and said to herself: "A fine bridge!"

She galloped out on the bridge, but when she reached the middle, the bridge broke and the Baba Yaga fell with a thud into the river, and there a cruel death overtook her!

Prince Ivan pastured the colt in green meadows, and he grew into a wonderful horse. Then the prince came riding up to Marya Morevna. She came running to meet him, threw herself on his neck, and said: "How did God deliver you?"

"So and so," said he; "come with me."

"I am afraid, Prince Ivan! If Koshchei should catch us, he would make mincemeat of you again."

"No, he will not catch us this time! I have a wonderful and a gallant horse; he flies like a bird."

They mounted on the horse's back and set off.

Koshchei the Deathless was on his way home; his horse stumbled under him.

"What is the matter with you, you hungry jade, that you stumble so? or do you scent some misfortune?"

"Prince Ivan has come and has carried off Marya Morevna."

"Well, we can catch him, can't we?"

"God knows! now Prince Ivan has a gallant horse, better than I am."

"I cannot help that," said Koshchei the Deathless. "I am going in pursuit of him."

Long, long he pursued Prince Ivan before he overtook him. Then he leaped to the ground and was just going to cut him with his keen sabre, but at that instant Prince Ivan's horse kicked Koshchei the Deathless with his hoof and split his head, and the prince finished him with his club. After this the prince piled wood on his chest, kindled a fire, and burnt Koshchei the Deathless on the pyre and he scattered the ashes to the winds.

Marya Morevna mounted on Koshchei's steed and Prince Ivan on his own, and they went first and visited the Raven, then the Eagle, and finally the Hawk. And wherever they came they were received with a joyous welcome:

"Oh, Prince Ivan, we never expected to see you again! But you have not been through all this trouble in vain; for such a beautiful woman as Marya Morevna you might seek throughout the whole world, but you would never find another!"

They feasted them, they entertained them, and then they came home to their own kingdom. When they got there they lived happily ever after.

THE FROG-QUEEN

ONCE upon a time a king and queen lived in a certain kingdom, in a certain realm, beyond blue seas, beyond high mountains. Long had the king lived in the white world, and as he lived he grew old, and to aid him he had three sons, three princes—all young men and so gallant that neither tongue could describe nor pen depict them. They used to go flying about the whole day long on their splendid steeds, like bright hawks through the sky. All three brothers were handsome and brave, but the best of them, the finest of them, was the youngest brother, and his name was Prince Ivan.

One day the king called his sons to him and said: "My dear children, you are now grown up. It is time for you to think of getting married. You shall have wives and I daughters-in-law. Let each choose a well-tempered arrow and go down into the forbidden meadow. Bend your stiff bows and shoot your arrows, and into whatever courtyard your arrows fall, there will you find your brides."

The oldest brother shot his arrow, and it fell into the yard of a rich noble, right over against the room occupied by the daughter of the house.

The second son shot his arrow, and it flew into the courtyard of a rich merchant, and remained sticking in the red stairway, and on the stairway stood the merchant's daughter.

Prince Ivan shot his arrow. It soared high, it fell out of sight, and though he hunted for it long he could not find it. So his heart grew heavy, and he was sad. For two whole days he wandered over the meadows and through the forests, but on the third day he made his way into a miry swamp, and he saw there a Frog, and the Frog had his arrow.

Prince Ivan was on the point of running away and leaving his arrow, but the Frog cried out:

"Kwa! kwa! Prince Ivan! Come to me and take your arrow, else you will never escape from the bog!"

There was no choice. Prince Ivan took the Frog, put her in the folds of his coat, and wended his way home. He went to his father and said:

"How can I marry a Frog? A Frog is n't my equal."

"There! there!" exclaimed the king, "this is only your fortune!"

Prince Ivan was very sad, and he shed many tears, but you see there is no resisting one's fate.

So the young princes were provided with wives. The oldest had the noble's daughter; the second had the merchant's daughter; while the youngest had to take for his wife the little Frog, and he kept her in a dish after they were married. And so they lived for some time.

But one day the king summoned his sons and give them this order: "Let your wives bake for my breakfast to-morrow some fresh white bread."

Prince Ivan went home to his palace in no happy frame of mind, and his proud head hung down below his shoulders.

"Kwa! kwa! Prince Ivan, why so troubled?" asked his Frog. "Did you hear a disagreeable word from your father?"

"How can I help being troubled? The sovereign, my father, has commanded that you furnish him with some fresh white bread for to-morrow."

"Do not be distressed, Prince Ivan; do not disturb yourself for nothing, but go to bed. Morning is cleverer than Evening."

She got the prince off to sleep, and then she laid

aside her frogskin. In her place stood the Soul-maiden, Vasilisa the All-wise, and so beautiful that neither tongue could describe nor pen depict her. She went to the stairway and called out in a loud voice:

"Maidies! maidies! come get the materials and make some fresh white bread, such as I used to eat when I lived in my own father's house!"

In the morning Prince Ivan woke up and found that the Frog had the bread all ready for him, and such fine bread as could not be imagined or conceived, but only described in a story. The loaf was adorned with different kinds of devices: on the sides were to be seen the king's cities and the gates.

Prince Ivan took the bread and carried it to his father, who had just received the loaves from the older brothers. Their wives had put them into the oven, and so they came out mere lumps of dough. First the king took the oldest son's loaf, glanced at it, and sent it to the kitchen; then he took the second son's bread and sent it there also. When it came Prince Ivan's turn he presented his bread. His father took it, looked at it, and exclaimed:

"Here is bread to eat on Easter — not half dough like that of my other daughters-in-law!"

Again the king gave this order to his three sons: "Let your wives make me a shirt in one night."

Prince Ivan went home in no happy frame of mind; his proud head hung down below his shoulders.

"Kwa kwa! Prince Ivan, why are you so troubled?" asked his Frog. "Can you have heard some sharp disagreeable word from your father?"

Prince Ivan replied: "How can I help being troubled? The sovereign, my father, has ordered me to provide him a new shirt in a single night."

"Do not be distressed, Prince Ivan. Do not disturb yourself for nothing: Morning is cleverer than Evening."

She got the prince off to sleep, and then she laid aside her frogskin and once more became the Soul-maiden, Vasilisa the All-wise, and so beautiful that neither tongue could describe nor pen depict her beauty. She went to the stairway and called out in a loud voice:

"Maidies! maidies! come and get the material and embroider a shirt such as my own father used to have made for him!"

No sooner said than done. In the morning when Prince Ivan woke up, his Frog had the shirt all ready, and such a wonderful shirt as could not be imagined or conceived, but only described in a story. It was decorated with gold and silver and clever designs. Prince Ivan took the shirt and carried it to his father. The king took it and looked at it: "Well, now, this is a shirt to wear on Easter Sunday!"

The second brother brought his shirt, when the king said: "I'd only go to the bath in that!" But when he took the elder brother's shirt, he said: "Take it to the kitchen!"

The king's sons departed, and the two elder ones said to each other: "It is plain we must n't laugh at Prince Ivan's wife; she is not a Frog, but some kind of a witch."

Again the king gave orders that all his three sons should appear at a ball with their wives. Prince Ivan went home to his palace in no happy frame of mind; his proud head hung down below his shoulders.

His Frog asked him: "Kwa! kwa! Prince Ivan, why so troubled? Did you hear a discourteous word from your father?"

Prince Ivan replied: "How can I help being troubled? The sovereign, my father, has commanded that I come with you to a ball at his palace. How can I show you to people?"

"Don't be distressed, prince! Go alone and mingle with the guests, and I will follow after. When you hear a knocking and a commotion, say: 'That is my Froggie come in her little box.'"

Well, then, the elder brothers went to the ball with their wives, in their very best clothes and all their ornaments, and they stood around and made sport of Prince Ivan.

"How is it with you, brother? Did you come without your wife? Or did you bring her in your handkerchief? And where did you find such a beauty? Say, did you search through all the bogs?"

Suddenly a great knocking and commotion was heard — the whole palace shook. The guests were frightened to death; they jumped from their places and did not know what to do. But Prince Ivan said: "Don't be afraid, friends! That is my Froggie come in her little box."

Up to the king's front steps came flying a golden coach drawn by six horses, and out of it stepped Vasilisa the All-wise — so beautiful that she could not be imagined or conceived, nor even described in a story. She took Prince Ivan by the hand and led him behind the oaken tables, behind the checked linen tablecloths.

The guests began to eat, drink, and be merry. Vasilisa the All-Wise drank from a glass and poured the dregs up her left sleeve. She ate some swan flesh and thrust some of the bones up her right sleeve. The wives of the two elder princes marvelled at her cleverness, and lo! they had to do the same thing!

Afterwards when Vasilisa the All-Wise went out to dance with Prince Ivan she shook her left sleeve — a lake was formed; she shook her right sleeve, and over the water flew white swans. The king and the guests were mightily astonished.

Now the two elder daughters-in-law started to dance. They shook their left sleeves — all they succeeded in doing was to spatter the other guests; they shook their right sleeves — a bone flew out and hit the king directly in the eye. The king was angry and sent them home in disgrace.

Meantime Prince Ivan seized his opportunity, ran home, found the frogskin, and burnt it up in a great fire. When Vasilisa the All-Wise came and discovered that her frogskin was gone, she grew sad and said to the prince:

"Oh, Prince Ivan, what have you done? If you had only waited a little I should have been yours forever. But now good-bye! You will find me beyond the thrice-nine lands, in the thirtieth kingdom, at the ends of the earth, with Koshchei the Deathless."

So saying, she turned into a white swan and flew out of the window.

Prince Ivan wept bitterly, but you see there was no help for it. For a whole year Prince Ivan longed for his wife. The next year he made up his mind, asked his father's permission and his mother's blessing, said his prayers to God, bowing to all four sides, and started forth whither eyes look.

He travelled far and near, he wandered up and down. At last he chanced to fall in with a little old man who accosted him:

"Your health, my dear lad! and what are you seeking for, and whither are you going?"

The prince told him about his misfortune.

"Eh! Prince Ivan, why did you burn up the frogskin? You did n't have to put it on, and you did n't have to take it off. Vasilisa the All-Wise was born cleverer and keener witted than her father. That was why he was angry with her and commanded her to be a frog for three years. Here is a little ball for you; wherever it rolls, follow it boldly."

Prince Ivan thanked the old man and started

after the little ball. He went along an open field and met with a bear.

"Hold on!" said he. "I will kill the beast."

But the Bear said to him: "Do not kill me, Prince Ivan; I may be useful to you some time."

So he went farther, and lo! a wild drake flew up. The prince aimed his arrow at him and was going to shoot the bird, when suddenly he said in a human voice:

"Do not kill me, Prince Ivan! Even I may be of use to you."

He heeded his request and went on his way. A squint-eyed hare ran out. The prince was again about to shoot his bow at him, but the Hare said in a human voice:

"Do not kill me, Prince Ivan. Even I may be useful to you."

Prince Ivan heeded his request and went on his way, till at last he came to the blue sea, and there he saw a sturgeon gasping on the beach.

"Ah! Prince Ivan," besought the Sturgeon, "have pity on me and put me back into the sea."

He threw her into the sea and then proceeded along the shore. As he went and went, the little ball rolled up to a small hut which stood on a hen's legs and turned round and round.

Prince Ivan said: "Little hut! little hut! stand as you used to — with your face to me and your back to the sea."

The little hut turned round with its back to the sea and faced him. Prince Ivan went in and saw on the stove, on the thrice-ninth brick, the Baba Yaga lying with her nose through the ceiling and grinding her teeth.

"Hello, you, young man! why have you come to me?" demanded the Baba Yaga of Prince Ivan.

"Oh you old hag!" he replied boldly, "you had better first give me something to eat and drink, and a good warm bath, before you ask questions of this young man!"

The Baba Yaga gave him food and drink and a warm bath, and then the prince told her that he was going in search of his wife Vasilisa the All-Wise.

"Oh, I know!" exclaimed the Baba Yaga. "She is now with Koshchei the Deathless. It is hard to reach her; it is not easy to overcome the immortal one: his death is on the end of a needle; the needle is in an egg; the egg is in a duck; the duck is in a hare; the hare is in a box; the box stands on a tall oak; and the tree is guarded by Koshchei like the apple of his eye."

The Baba Yaga showed him in what place that oak

was growing. Prince Ivan went there and did not know what he should do or how to reach the box. Suddenly, coming from somewhere, appeared a bear and he uprooted the tree. The box fell out and broke to pieces; the hare ran out of the box and scampered away with all its might and main. But behold! a second hare darted after it, overtook it, and tore it into bits. Out of the hare flew a duck and went high, high into the air. She flew away, but behind her in full pursuit darted a drake, and as soon as he overtook her the duck dropped an egg, and the egg fell into the sea.

Prince Ivan, seeing misfortune, wept bitter tears; but suddenly a sturgeon swam up to the shore holding the egg in her teeth. Prince Ivan took it, broke it, took out the needle, and broke off the point. How Koshchei struggled, and how he struck out in all directions — but he had to die!

Prince Ivan went to Koshchei's house, took Vasilisa the All-Wise, and went home. After this they lived together and were happy ever after.